KU-442-921

TOP
SECRET

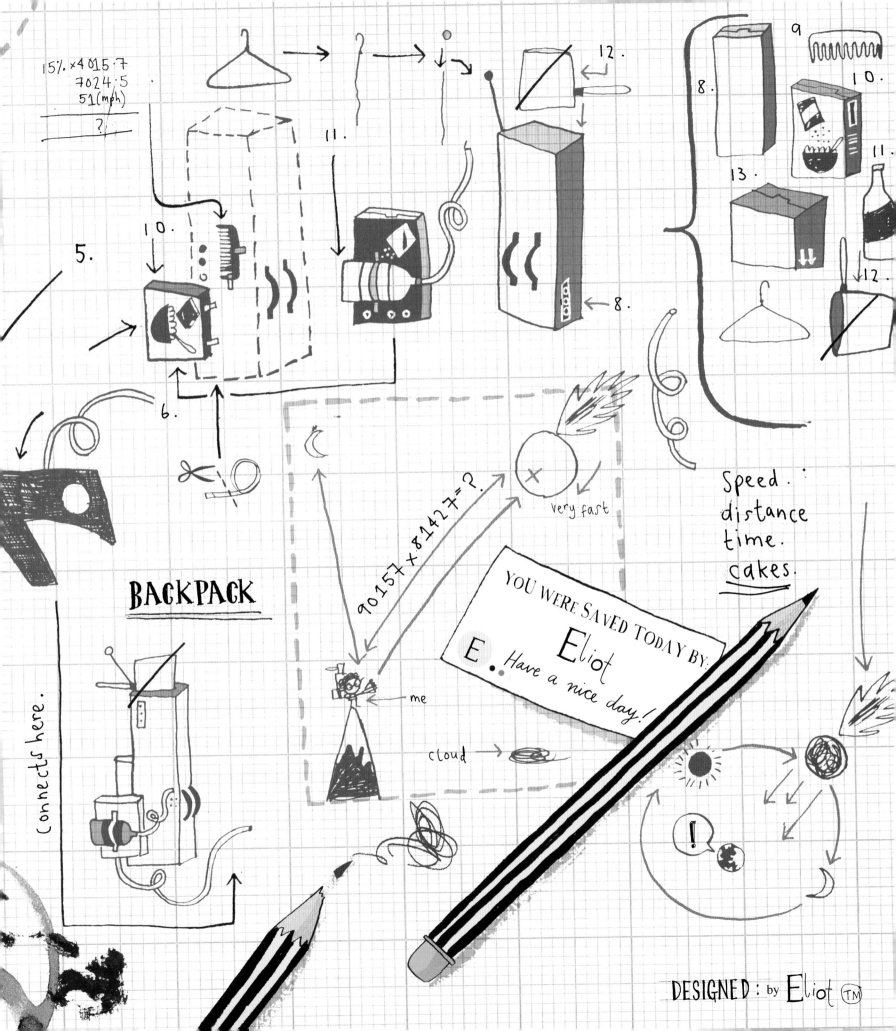

For my three forever superheroes, Richard, Joe and Freddy – A.C.

For my heroes, Georgia, Thomas and Jemma – A.T.S

First published as *Eliot Jones, Midnight Superhero* in
2008 by Scholastic Children's Books
This edition first published in 2013
by Scholastic Children's Books
Euston House, 24 Eversholt Street
London NW1 1DB
a division of Scholastic Ltd
www.scholastic.co.uk
London ~ New York ~ Toronto ~ Sydney
~ Auckland ~ Mexico City ~ New Delhi ~ Hong Kong

Text copyright © 2008 Anne Cottringer
Illustrations copyright © 2008 Alex T. Smith

PB ISBN 978 1407 13916 6

All rights reserved
Printed in Malaysia

10 9 8 7 6 5 4 3 2

The moral rights of Anne Cottringer and Alex T. Smith have been asserted.

Papers used by Scholastic Children's Books are made from wood grown in sustainable forests.

Eliot
MIDNIGHT SUPERHERO

SCHOLASTIC

By day,
Eliot is quiet.
He reads his books.
He feeds his goldfish.
He watches Mr Smith
wash his car.

TIBET

TOY BOX

"Eliot is such a quiet little thing," say all the grownups.

Tick! Tock! Tick! Tock! Tick! Tock!

BONG!

But when the clock strikes *midnight*...

Eliot is a Superhero!

He hangs out of
helicopters.

He skis down glaciers.

He returns teddies
to babies.

Eliot

Sometimes the mayor needs Eliot's help.

"The lions have escaped from the zoo!" he cries. "They're rampaging through the streets!"

Luckily, Eliot is an expert lion tamer.

He leaps from his bedroom window, races through the screaming crowds...

…and comes face to face with the lions.
He stares into the eyes of the
ROARING beasts.

One by one,
    Eliot stops them
        in their tracks.

He leads the
    lions back
    to the zoo...

...as the
    crowds cheer.

Sometimes the
Coast Guard call
on his services.

"Help!" they shout.
"A ship is about to CRASH
onto the rocks!"

Luckily, Eliot is a
champion swimmer.

THE RUBBER DUCKY

He dives into the towering waves,
grabs the anchor and tows the ship to safety,
as the sailors shout "Hurray!"

Sometimes the Queen requires his assistance. "A criminal mastermind has **stolen** the royal jewels!" announces the Royal Butler.

Luckily, Eliot is an excellent sleuth.

He sneaks into the criminal mastermind's secret hideout.

Tip-toe!

He follows the clues, cracks the code, opens the safe...

...and returns the jewels to the grateful Queen.

Tonight, Eliot receives an urgent message from the world's Most Important Scientists.

"A gigantic METEOR is heading this way! It's going to SMASH into the Earth!"

This is Eliot's most important mission ever!

Luckily, Eliot has built a Meteor-Busting
Rocket Launcher for just such occasions.

Unluckily, it's hidden in a deep cave in the mountains of **TIBET** .

The only way to get there before the meteor strikes is by supersonic jet.
Luckily, Eliot is a skilled jet pilot.

Eliot sets off.
Over the Alps.
Over the Caspian Sea.
Across to the Himalayas.

RUSSIA

ARABIAN SEA

TREASURE!

INDIAN OCEAN

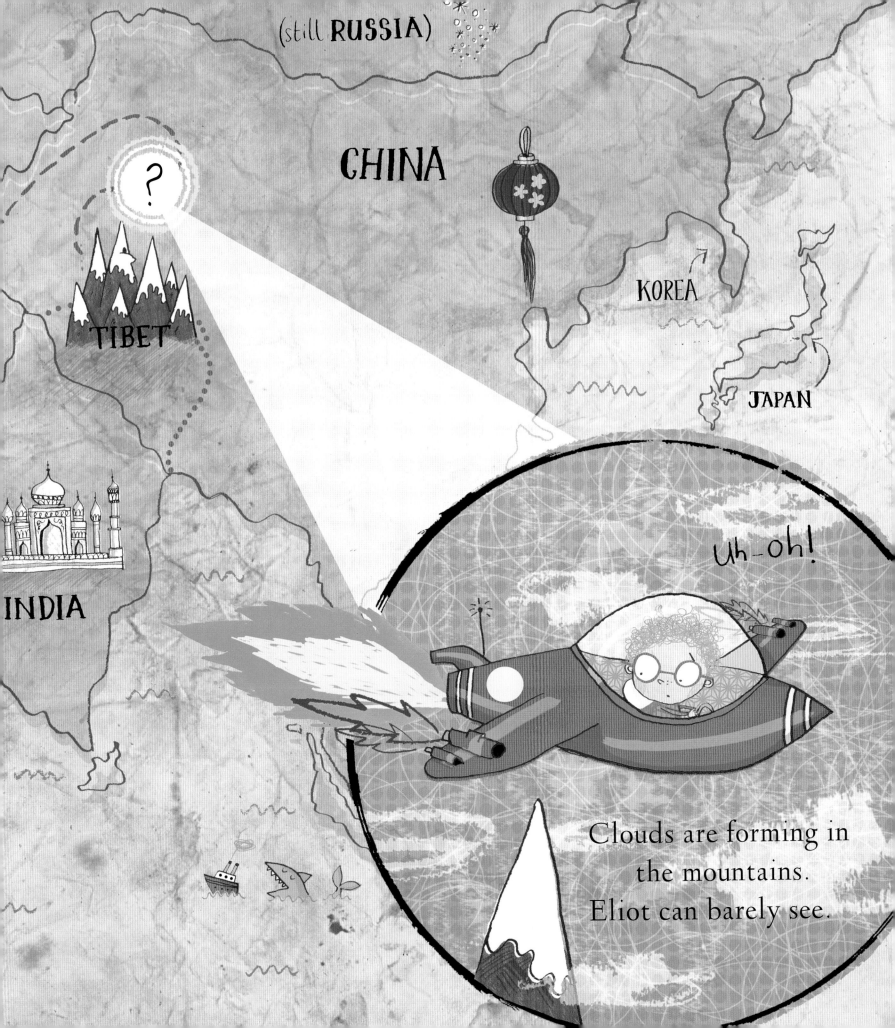

Suddenly a snow-capped peak
flashes past his window.
Another looms up straight ahead.
Eliot dips his left wing
and swerves just in time.

To reach the cave he must now
land on the shortest,
most dangerous
runway in the world.

He grips
the controls.
The wheels
bump the ground.

Screeech!
Eliot skids to a halt.

The sky is blazing with
the light of the meteor.

Closer
and
closer
it comes.

Eliot can see the entrance
to the cave, far above him.
Luckily, Eliot is a highly
experienced mountaineer.
He scrambles up the cliff face,
and into the cave.

Eliot swings the barrel of the
Meteor-Busting Rocket
Launcher towards the sky.

He aims.
He holds his breath.
He waits until just
the right moment...

He fires! KAPOW!

Eliot saves the world from destruction!

The Queen gives Eliot an award for his courage and ingenuity.

The Earth trembles with deafening applause.

TOY BOX

TIBET

But being a
    Midnight Superhero
is very tiring.

It doesn't leave Eliot
    with much energy.
So by day...

Eliot is quiet.

TOP SECRET

1.
2.
3.
4.
7.
a
b
c

$x\sqrt{\dfrac{3 \times 2}{18}}$

3·950
× 8·19.

powered by:

CARDBOARD

draw · cut out · stick

$2+2+2+2=8$

$y\sqrt{8+10087219}$

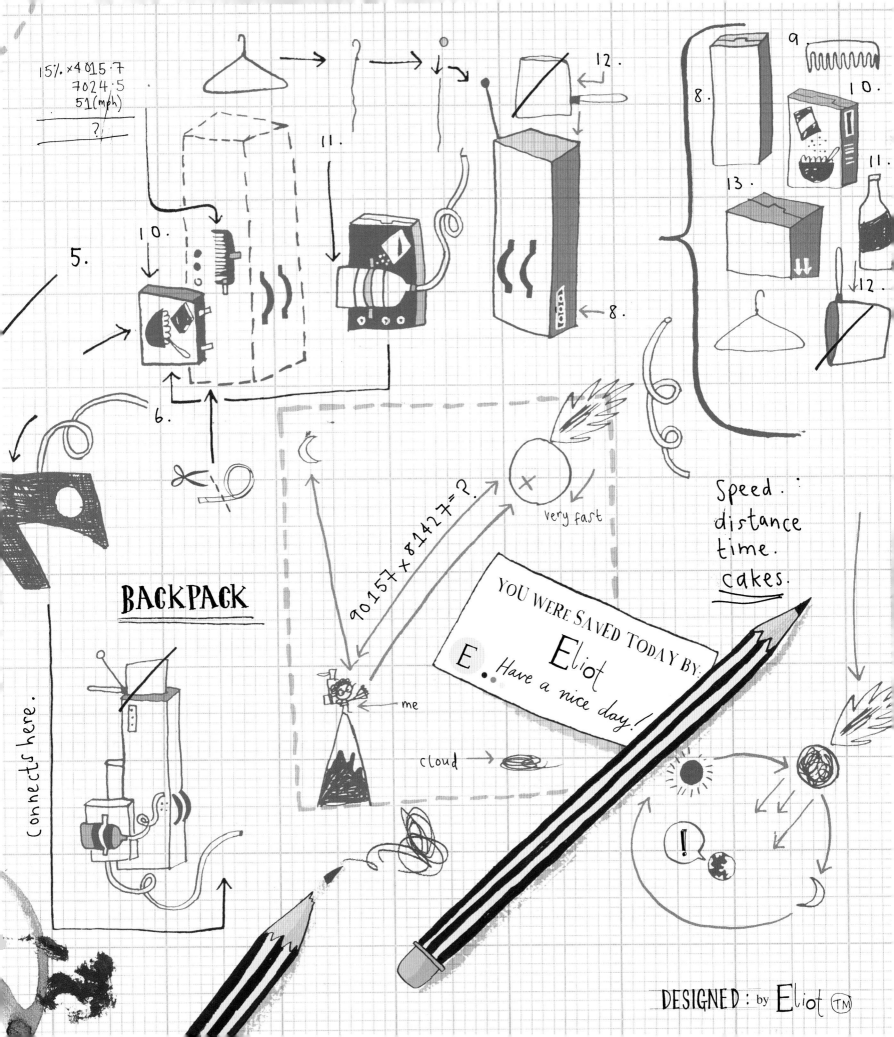